MARCO POLO

MARCO POLO
Dangers and Visions

Marco Tabilio

Translation by Kerstin Schwandt

Graphic Universe™ • Minneapolis

First American edition published in 2017 by Graphic Universe™

Copyright © by Marco Tabilio
Copyright © 2015 by BeccoGiallo S.r.l. for the Italian edition.

Published in arrangement with AMBook (www.ambook.ch)

Translation by Kerstin Schwandt
English translation © 2017 by Lerner Publishing Group, Inc.

Graphic Universe™ is a trademark of Lerner Publishing Group, Inc.

Graphic Universe™
A division of Lerner Publishing Group, Inc
241 First Avenue North
Minneapolis, MN 55401 USA

For reading levels and more information, look up this title at
www.lernerbooks.com.

Main body text set in King George Bold Clean 9/9.
Typeface provided by Chank.

Library of Congress Cataloging-in-Publication Data

Names: Tabilio, Marco, author.
Title: Marco Polo : dangers and visions / Marco Tabilio; translated by
   Kerstin Schwandt.
Description: First North American edition. | Minneapolis : Graphic Universe,
   2017. | Includes bibliographical references.
Identifiers: LCCN 2016006055 (print) | LCCN 2016010077 (ebook) | ISBN
   9781512411829 (lb : alk. paper) | ISBN 9781512427028 (eb pdf)
Subjects: LCSH: Polo, Marco, 1254-1323?—Juvenile literature. | Explorers-
   -Italy—Biography—Juvenile literature. | Travel, Medieva—Juvenile
   literature. | Asia—Description and trave—Juvenile literature.
Classification: LCC G370.P9 T34 2017 (print) | LCC G370.P9 (ebook) | DDC
   915.04/2092 [B] —dc23

LC record available at https://lccn.loc.gov/2016006055

Manufactured in the United States of America
1-39682-21295-1/9/2017

少小離家老大回
鄉音無改鬢毛衰
兒童相見不相識
笑問客從何處來

I was young when I left home.

I came back older but carefree.

My accent has not changed much,

but my hair much thinner be.

Now those I meet know not my face.

They ask, "From whence come thee?"

He Zhizhang (ca. 659–744), *Coming Home*

8

14

Genoa, Italy, 1298

23

I spent my youth at the port.

Trabzon

Persia

Alexandria

Genoa

Ragusa

silk

turmeric

pepper

cumin

Hey! What do you think you're doing?

Nothing.

You came from Sudak, right? Have you heard any news about Niccolo Polo?

Nobody ever knew anything. I was two years old when my father went to Constantinople as a trader.

Who raised you?

My mother. While she was alive.

Then a sister of my father, Aunt Flora, and her husband, Gianni.

They loved me, and I loved them. I didn't stand out, but I never made any trouble.

Mostly, I kept to myself.

27

My feet were in the lagoon, but
my eyes looked out to sea.

I listened to the tales
of the merchants. I
could tell what port
they were from just
by looking at them.

Even at the port in Venice, I could
sense the presence of the East,
but it was insulated, hidden away,
like a bather behind the reeds.

And then a piece
of me, once lost there,
was returned.

41

russia

moscow

the golden horde

kipchak khanate

kieu

venice

PAX TIBI MAR CE

soldaia

saraj

berke khan

trabzon

black sea

michael viii palaiologos

constantinople

caspian sea

palazzo

acri

herat

jerusalem

bag...

THE FIRST VOYAGE OF NICCOLO
AND MAFFEO POLO, 1261-1265

The day of departure was sunny.

But everything was still wet from days of rain.

Taking my last looks at Venice, I saw only the reflection of sunlight on the wet streets.

I said good-bye to the aunt and uncle I was close to.

Zanin, if you're good, I'll bring you a present when I come back.

I didn't know when I'd see them again.

We embarked on the large galley of merchants, heading to St. John d'Acre.

Then—days of sea and silence. Now I understand why travelers are quiet. When a man leaves the land, he leaves spoken words behind.

My father didn't say a thing to me the entire trip.

Did your father punish you for saying that?

No. Well, maybe...

Perhaps it was not entirely appropriate.

Anyway—it was a little before Easter, and St. John d'Acre was full of people. Innkeepers, soldiers, smugglers, merchants, nuns.

What stuck out to you the most?

The pilgrims, I think.

They are treated like rags, moved around and housed in terrible conditions. They have to pay for everything.

They are robbed at least once a week.

But they always have such enthusiasm. It's impossible to get them down.

And they sell these little items to devotees. Lions, holy cards.

I bought one myself, on the way to Jerusalem.

SAN CRISTOFORO

Now, Jerusalem—what can I tell you about the city that you don't already know?

The garden of olive trees, the tomb, the crucifixion site?

The Temple of Solomon and the magnificent mosques of stone and gold?

The old walls and the intermingling of chants, bells, and prayer calls?

Jerusalem etches itself in your body for a lifetime.

And the city is exactly how you imagine it. Street by street, tower by tower.

CHURCH OF THE
HOLY SEPULCHER

political map of the

HOLY LAND

We set out. From that moment on, there would be no distractions.

We went toward Cathay, toward the Great Khan.

The pope had provided two wise Dominican friars.

They weren't all the khan had asked for, but at least they were something.

The elder was Guglielmo from Tripoli, a taciturn man. He wanted to write a book on the East.

The young man, we knew already.

Wherever we were, these two priests would officiate a quick Mass every morning before breakfast.

I was never devout, I must confess. But traveling with those two men still gave me comfort.

*It's not that he keeps track, but the fact is that this is not the first time Guglielmo has seen things that don't exist. This worries the Dominican from Tripoli.

**Guglielmo has never mentioned his visions to anybody. In fact, only a few years ago, he publicly mocked an old sexton, claiming the elder man was not quite right in the head.

Baibars, the sultan of Egypt, had moved with a mighty army against Little Armenia.

His warriors were moving northward, crushing whoever opposed them.

This is what the man told Guglielmo.

May we speak with you?

We cannot continue.

I didn't think it would be like this.

I'm sorry. I do apologize. But we must go back.

I have to follow Guglielmo.

We'll take refuge at a fortress of the Templars.

I had just found a friend and lost him just as quickly.

Men at the ports would say that the Mongols learn to ride before walking.

They are deadly warriors. They do not fight covered in iron, like our soldiers. They bring with them only bows, arrows, and light swords.

Nothing can wear them down.

Riding days without stopping, through the wastelands and hot deserts, they get almost no sleep.

They eat little. Just meat and fermented milk from the horses.

When there is nothing to eat, a warrior opens the vein of his horse and drinks the blood.

We have been born into an age of fear.

For a time, the shadow of the Mongols fell on Latin lands.

They had already crushed the Christian kingdoms of eastern Europe with massacres, rapes, and arson.

The churches were filled. Priests called their followers to repent and predicted the arrival of the Day of Judgment.

If asked, anyone would answer with certainty that it was the advent of the Antichrist.

Then the horde stopped. As if a miracle had occurred.

Having imposed their order in Asia, the Mongols opened all the trade routes, like uncorking a keg.

And trade began to flow, though a great fear of the Mongols lingered. Superstitions passed among traders as easily as goods: headless men, men with the heads of dogs.

While on the Silk Road, some merchants imagined themselves to be always under the Mongols' watch— all-seeing, bigger than life.

DIVISION OF THE BODY OF
GENGHIS KHAN AFTER HIS DEATH

ARMENIA

GEORGIA   MOSUL

THE FALL OF
BAGHDAD, 1258

Baghdad is a big and beautiful city, Rustichello, but a traveler there is only seeing a shadow.

The splendid city was shattered by Hulagu Khan, the brother of Kublai.

One hundred thousand men, the largest Mongol army ever assembled.

Tigers stroll across the grounds.

Alongside the ghost of the great library.

In the streets, ghosts and the living walk together.

During the siege, the river became black with the ink of a thousand library books dumped into the water and red with the blood of the scientists and philosophers killed.

You wanted to keep these treasures, instead of paying mercenaries to fight me?

Enjoy them now.

Hulagu closed the caliph of Baghdad in a tower and let him starve.

Fine horses and
fantastic donkeys

Aharasan

Zinc oxide
mines

Aubanan

Silk, muslin,
and gold

Best drapery
and silk weaving

tabriz

mosul

Magnificent
cloth, superb
wild donkeys

Turquoise
and steel

Aerman

**Loot desert of
Airman**

City of the caliph,
decorated with
beasts and birds

Baghdad

Basra

Yazd

camadi

Spices, elephants,
date wine (careful,
it's a laxative),
harsh air

Best dates
in the world

Dates, pistachio
nuts, bananas,
white oxen, sheep
as big as donkeys

Aormuz

Aish

What else? There's a thick, dark oil that slides out from certain pools in the earth.

It's common to see it when traveling in Persia along the Silk Road.

The oil is horrible to look at and doesn't smell good either.

But many men make the trip to bring some back to the city.

Some think it has healing powers.

The men traveling past an expanse of trees...

...can use the oil to make fires there.

It burns very well.

But it makes very dark smoke.

We stink something awful! We'd better change clothes.

The smoke covered Uncle Maffeo until we reached the Persian city of Saveh.

The three wise men are buried in those lands, still with their beards and everything.

They brought gold to the Christ Child to see if he was a god, incense to see if he was a king, and myrrh to see if the king was a magician.

But when they arrived with these gifts, each man saw a face, similar to his own.

They all recognized him for what he was: a thirteen-day-old child.

Christ received the gifts and gave the three wise men a box.

As the men carried it home, it became increasingly heavy.

They decided to open it. But it contained only a plain stone.

Disappointed, they threw it into a pit, but a pillar of fire came down from heaven.

Since then, fire has been worshipped in these parts.

And many people await the passage of the three wise men.

A traveler who enters the steppe of Khorasan will find, in a certain place, a large tree.

It's called the Lone Tree. Some say the tree will bloom on Judgment Day.

Others recall a great battle that Alexander the Great fought near the tree.

Its foliage is green on the top and white underneath. It produces a lot of chestnuts, but they are always empty.

99

As we rode, my uncle told me about the old man of the mountain, the one our curious friend had mentioned.

He was the leader of a sect of assassins. He kidnapped nearby children. He drugged them with opium and had them wake up in a wonderful garden.

The old man told them that they were in paradise.

There were flowers, streams, juicy fruits. Girls playing sweet melodies.

When the old man wanted to eliminate a rival...

...one of the young assassins would wake up outside of paradise, holding a piece of paper with the victim's name.

He would seek him out and kill him mercilessly.

Then he would be readmitted.

But the Mongols destroyed the assassins long ago. I didn't have the heart to tell that young man.

That young man will remain inconsolable for a long time.

113

BALKH   TALOQAN

123

The Wakhan is the name of a land squeezed between high mountains.

The nomads who live there call it the Roof of the World.

The mountain chains of Karakorum, the Pamir, and the Hindu Kush dominate a traveler's view, like a constant thought.

We went to the
rock walls, where
monk healers live in
hermitages above the
emptiness.

We climbed the
Pamir Mountains.

Flocks of sheep and
wolves roamed the area.

Bones and horns were piled up
in the drifts of snow.

When I recovered, I realized
that I had changed. I had
a new face.

There was new hair on my
head. And I was taller by a foot.

I tried out my new body
on the way down from
the mountains.

Lop is the last outpost before a vast desert.

Passing through it takes a year of walking in desolation.

The traveler must rest a week before moving along the bed of the White Jade River.

In the desert, you sometimes think you hear voices calling or the drums of a huge army around you. It's enough to drive you mad or make you turn around.

That leg of the journey lasts a month. One month of feeling like the walking dead.

Kashgar

Yarkant

Karglik

Lop

Khotan

In the province of Tangut, ritual dictates that the deceased are kept at home for several days...

turfan

Homul

Khara Khoto

TANGUT

...covered with saffron and spices so that the body doesn't smell until the soothsayers decide on a day.

Then the body is brought to the funeral pyre and burned along with its possessions and animals. These will accompany the person after death.

Dunhuang

Gobi desert

Chinese empire of
the Great Khan

Shangdu.
The heavenly
encampment.

The khan and his court
spent the summer months
in Shangdu to escape the
heat of Khanbaliq.

A city of tents and the most splendid city imaginable.

The Mongols built the city in the style of what they considered paradise.

There is endless green and blue in every direction.

Khanbaliq.

The capital of the khan became my home for the following years.

Kublai sent me around the different provinces of the empire, but at the end of each mission, I always came back to Khanbaliq.

I did everything for the emperor.

Hunting companion

Imperial messenger

Interpreter (Persian, Latin, Tartar)

Geographer

Caravan leader

Tax collector

Foreman

Supervisor at the mines

Controller of the water supply

Ambassador

Spy

Master salt extractor

Adviser to the fisheries

Courier

Merchant (as always)

Supervisor at
the mint

Religious mediator

Conductor of imperial
examinations

Officer of charity

Philosopher
(improvised)

Storyteller

Consultant to
the emperor

Friend

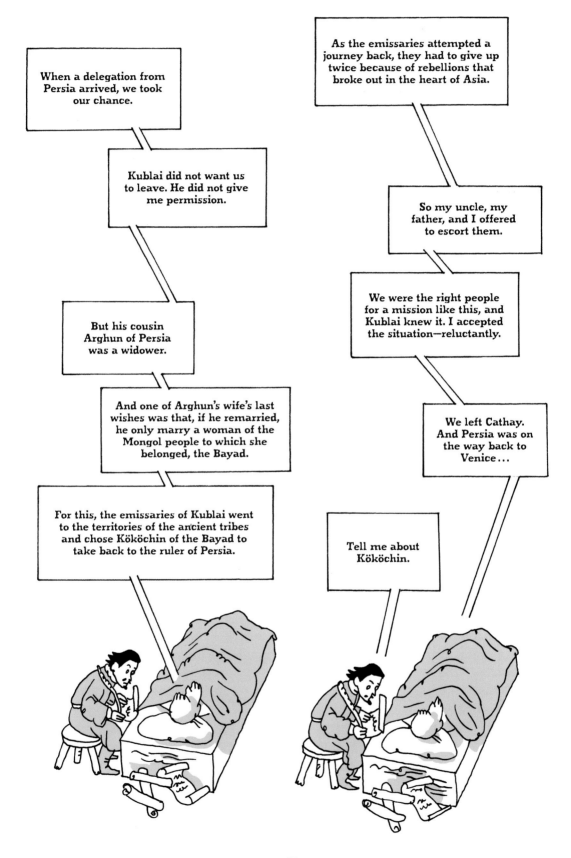

When a delegation from Persia arrived, we took our chance.

Kublai did not want us to leave. He did not give me permission.

But his cousin Arghun of Persia was a widower.

And one of Arghun's wife's last wishes was that, if he remarried, he only marry a woman of the Mongol people to which she belonged, the Bayad.

For this, the emissaries of Kublai went to the territories of the ancient tribes and chose Kököchin of the Bayad to take back to the ruler of Persia.

As the emissaries attempted a journey back, they had to give up twice because of rebellions that broke out in the heart of Asia.

So my uncle, my father, and I offered to escort them.

We were the right people for a mission like this, and Kublai knew it. I accepted the situation—reluctantly.

We left Cathay. And Persia was on the way back to Venice...

Tell me about Kököchin.

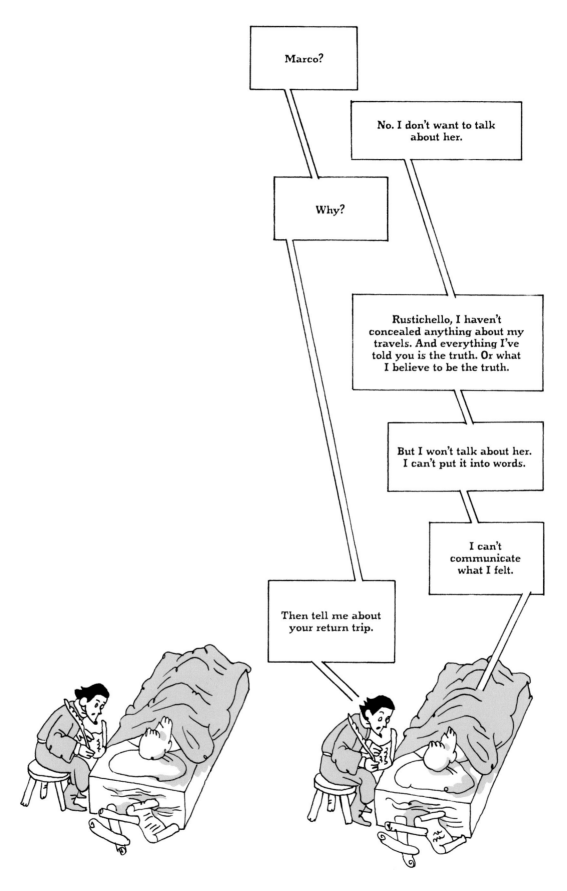

This is the chronicle of my journey back. We started in 1290, with the aim of bringing the princess Kököchin to the sovereign of the Tatars of Persia, and ended in 1295 in Venice.

We stayed on the island of Sumatra for five months, because a storm came and it didn't stop raining all that time.

We disassembled two ships and built a small, fortified city to defend ourselves from any hostile people or man-eating beasts.

For five months, we ate a diet of fish, coconuts, and palm wine.

There, we heard that if local soothsayers deem a dying man incurable, he is killed and then cooked by his family.

Everything is eaten, even the marrow. They say that if anything is left over, the worms will develop a taste for it. But when the worms finish, they'll be out of food and die of starvation.

For this reason, they consume their dead: for the love of worms.

Leaving the Andaman Islands, sailing a thousand miles to the west and southwest, we came across the island of Ceylon.

It's home to quantities of rubies, topaz, sapphires, and amethysts like you've never seen.

The king of Ceylon has an enormous ruby, without a single flaw. Kublai once tried in vain to buy it, offering enough wealth for an entire city.

On this island, there is a mountain with a tomb.

The Muslims say that Adam is buried there, but the Buddhists say it's actually the tomb of Prince Siddhartha Gautama.

He was the son of a rich king, but he refused all wealth, all the women, and all the servants that his father wanted to surround him with to protect him from the fear of death.

And he lived in poverty, so humbly that—if he were here today—he would have been made a saint.

He was seeking a way to overcome death. And he succeeded, if what they say is true—that he lived eighty-four reincarnations, from ox to dog and, eventually, God.

...Doctor, he has started to ramble.

HORMUZ

The people of India wear little, living under immense heat. The king himself wears a collar, bracelets, and leggings made of precious jewels. Five hundred women live within his palace.

Here, when a man dies, it is considered the highest honor for a widow to throw herself on the funeral pyre and let herself burn.

The pearl divers pay snake charmers to charm the sharks while they fish.

Along India's west coast, we once again lost ships and men. This time because of pirates. Our numbers had already dwindled due to disease, storms, and desertions.

166

My father, my uncle, Kököchin, and I were among the living. We entered the lands of the khan of Persia.

We had not yet entered the capital of Tabriz when the news came.

Arghun Khan was dead.

Kököchin was a widow before she could even be married.

Arghun had died in the days when we departed from Cathay, two years earlier.

The throne of Persia was occupied by Gaikatu, brother of the deceased.

He arranged for a marriage between Kököchin and Arghun's son, the young Prince Ghazan.

Venice, 1297. One year prior to the imprisonment of Marco Polo.

Admiral Andrea Dandolo of Venice.

It's me. And you are Marco Polo, returning from the East.

Yes, Signore.

What is your wish, Messer Polo?

Admiral, I would like the honor of commanding a ship.

You know that the Genovese are moving against us.

They've dared to come here, to our Adriatic Sea.

Yes, Admiral. I want to fight against those wretches.

You're brave. That's good.

But it won't be easy. Death will be your companion.

I don't know any better company.

hopefully Death comes to get us soon
because I can't wait any longer

So be it. You'll command a galley. We sail tomorrow.

September 5, 1298.

September 8, 1298

THE FINAL DREAM OF MARCO POLO

In a quarter century of adventure
and danger in the East, I never hurt
anyone, not even in self-defense.

Now, I've killed people, and
for a miserable war between
miserable factions.

And perhaps I
myself am dead.

In the end, would
my death count for
anything?

Marco Polo
1254–1324

A traveler, a merchant, and a diplomat, Marco Polo journeyed to China and later wrote about it in the book *Il Milione* (also known as *The Travels of Marco Polo* and *Book of the Marvels of the World*). He sought to document the cultural practices, economies, politics, and histories of different countries of the Middle Ages. Over the centuries, his travelogue has been a source of inspiration and debate for writers, travelers, geographers, and scholars.

Marco Polo was born in 1254 in Venice. At that time, maritime republics (coastal city-states) were an economic and political force in the Mediterranean. Venetian merchant ships and military ships, with their Lion of Saint Mark banners, represented power and wealth throughout the Mediterranean colonies. Each Mediterranean port included a large Venetian quarter, an enclave where the merchants of Venice practiced their trade. Separate quarters also existed for Genoa, Pisa, and other maritime republics.

Before Marco Polo's birth, the Venetian Republic enjoyed a long-standing relationship with Constantinople (later known as Istanbul, Turkey), the era's largest and wealthiest European city. However, Constantinople was also troubled by uprisings; power in the city changed hands multiple times throughout the thirteenth century. Around 1260 Niccolo and Maffeo Polo—Venetian merchants and the father and uncle of Marco Polo— were living in the town of Sudak along the Black Sea. They owned warehouses in the town's Venetian quarter. Hearing news of violence perpetrated against the Venetians in Constantinople—otherwise a natural stop on a return to Italy—they planned a trading expedition in the opposite direction, turning their eyes toward the East.

Niccolo and Maffeo made their way to Saraj, the capital of the Mongol khanate of the Golden Horde. There, they became acquainted with a delegation from another khanate, the Ilkhanate of Persia, and headed toward Kublai Khan's China (also known as Cathay). The Mongols were the dominant power in Asia at this time. After Genghis Khan united all the Mongol peoples under his command and annexed large parts of the continent, his descendants had continued the expansion, leading their forces through military conquests throughout almost all of Asia. Mongol territories extended to the edge of Europe. Over time, a political structure stabilized across the different Mongol khanates and travel along Asia's Silk Road—a network of trade routes—became easier.

Niccolo and Maffeo Polo entered into the service of Kublai Khan, the emperor of China— the most advanced and most prosperous land in the world. Kublai Khan asked them to visit the pope and to bring back a delegation of one hundred Christian wise men to serve in his court.

Tasked with this mission, the two Polo men began their return to Venice in 1265. They arrived in 1269. Marco, then in his mid-teens, met his father for the first time since Niccolo had left, when Marco was only two years old. Marco had grown up in a Venice that represented an open door to the East. Many languages echoed throughout the city's ports, and both foreign goods and amazing stories from the East were passed among the merchants. In the Middle Ages, the men and women of Europe lacked reliable information about Asia and imagined the continent as a place of wonders and monstrosities. Tall tales of the continent were common: cities of gold, men without heads, enormous-eared panotti, dogs that walked on two legs, dragons, basilisks, huge birds of prey, and sea monsters. These stores alternated between the obscene and the sublime, reflecting the anxieties and hopes of Europe during this period.

Marco Polo joined his father and his uncle on the road back to the East. The journey began in 1271. It was full of obstacles from the beginning. Between the death of Pope Clement IV and continually delayed election of a new pope, Christianity was in transition. The indecision lasted 1,006 days, the longest period to date in church history in which the papal throne remained vacant, and it culminated in the so-called fury of Viterbo. The citizens of Viterbo, a city that was then the papal seat, were exasperated by the endless deliberation over the new pope. They decided to literally lock up the cardinals in the palace, and they removed part of the roof to speed the cardinals along.

The election occurred while Niccolo, Maffeo, and Marco Polo were already en route, having reached Palestine. They made a short detour to meet Pope Gregory X, who was in St. John d'Acre, one of the crusader territories of the Holy Land. The Polos acquired the oil of the Holy Sepulcher of Jerusalem and a set of Christian scholars (not one hundred men but two Dominican friars: Nicholas of Vicenza and William of Tripoli) to take to Kublai. However, the Dominicans soon broke away from the company, and the three Polos continued onward by themselves. With help from golden coins that identified them as emissaries of the khan, they crossed into Georgia, Armenia, Persia, Afghanistan, the mountains protecting China, and the desert lands of Xinjiang. The Polos then traveled along a string of cities that led into the heart of the empire. After three years of traveling, they finally met Kublai in Shangdu in 1274. At Kublai's invitation, the Polos followed him to Khanbaliq (known in modern times as Beijing), the capital of his dynasty. Their arrival took place during a period of change and expansion for the Mongol Empire.

As the Polos began to serve the Great Khan in the role of imperial officials, Marco Polo, in his early twenties, stood out as a skilled observer and diplomat. His role grew due to his favor with the emperor. Marco traveled to the remote provinces of the khan's vast empire and to lands that had been freshly acquired. He became a witness to China's technological advancements during this period. A vast network of channels promoted the transport of goods and people, and also guaranteed rich, orderly agricultural production. The empire's many bridges and roads allowed people to move quickly between cultural centers. Its efficient economy led to abundant trade opportunities.

During the nearly two decades in which the Polos stayed in China, Marco and his relatives maintained prestigious positions in the court of the Great Khan. However, an opportunity to leave came around 1291. The khan of Persia, Arghun, a relative of the Great Khan, was a widower. He had to remarry a woman of proper lineage, from one of the original Mongol tribes stationed in the territories of Kublai. A delegation from Khanbaliq had selected Kököchin of the Bayad as the future wife of Arghun. Marco, Niccolo, and Maffeo Polo were given the difficult task of accompanying the princess and delegates to Persia. They would make the journey back to Venice thereafter.

The Polos, Kököchin, and members of the Persian khanate sailed with fourteen ships from the Chinese port of Quanzhou. In the course of their journey, they docked at Sumatra, Java, Ceylon (Sri Lanka), the west coast of India, and Hormuz on the Persian Gulf. Marco Polo's travelogues provide descriptions and observations about these places, as well as reports on what he was told about other places bordering the Indian Ocean, such as the East African coast.

Upon reaching Persia, the group learned that Arghun, Kököchin's betrothed, had died. Arghun's brother Gaikatu had seized power in a coup, taking advantage of Arghun's son, Ghazan. To avoid further problems in the area, Kököchin wed Ghazan. The Polos were able to make their journey to Venice thereafter. But new setbacks emerged: Marco and his fellow travelers were no longer able to rely on Christian ports throughout the Holy Land, because St. John d'Acre, the last of the territories controlled by European crusaders, fell in 1295 after a bloody siege by the Egyptian Mamluk forces of al-Ashraf Khalil. All Christian kingdoms in Palestine were dismantled. The Polos were forced to take a route through the area presently known as Turkey. In Trabzon, on the Black Sea, pirates—or perhaps Genovese marauders—robbed them of money and valuables. Later, they sailed through Negroponte (the island of Euboea in the Aegean Sea, a Venetian colony at the time). Marco, Niccolo, and Maffeo Polo finally reached Venice in 1295.

The three travelers found Europe changed, with a new balance of power in the Mediterranean. The upheavals in the Middle East, with Christian crusaders' strongholds disappearing, led to a more difficult trading culture. Venice also faced increased competition from Genoa, leading to armed conflict between the two Italian republics.

A formation of ninety-five Venetian war galleys took off from Venice to challenge the Genovese. One of these ships, traveling along the Dalmatian Coast, was commanded by Marco Polo. On September 8, 1298, the Venetian galleys met the Genovese fleet near Korčula, an island off the Adriatic Sea. The Genovese, though outnumbered, were able to break the ranks of the Venetian formation, at the cost of heavy casualties. The Battle of Korčula ended in a complete defeat for the Venetians. The vast majority of their galleys were sunk, seven thousand soldiers died, and at least as many were taken prisoner. Among the prisoners were Admiral Andrea Dandolo, who died immediately after his capture, and Marco Polo. In the Genovese prison, Marco Polo met Rustichello, a writer from Pisa. Rustichello may have been there since the Battle of Meloria, a 1284 conflict in which the Genovese attacked the Tuscans. The two began collaborating on an account of Marco Polo's travels.

The text, originally written in Old French, was immediately popular and sparked enthusiasm and controversy. It was widely read, transcribed, and translated, and it remains the subject of study and debate, as many of Marco Polo's claims have been disputed. Some accounts within *Il Milione* may reflect Polo's own biases or misunderstandings. Other accounts may have taken on the biases of editors or translators in the years after Polo conferred with Rustichello.

The influence of *Il Milione* can be found in the literature of later centuries. Christopher Columbus also consulted its pages in search of information about the peoples of India and China. The enigmatic title of the work could refer to the multitude of wonders Marco spoke of. *Il Milione* could also be derived from Emilione, one of the nicknames of a branch of the Polo family.

Marco Polo was freed from his Genovese prison in 1299. He returned to Venice, devoting himself to reworking and refining his travelogue. He settled into a peaceful life after marrying Donata Badoer in 1300, managing his considerable assets, and living in Venice's San Giovanni Grisostomo area. Marco Polo died on January 8, 1324.

A Traveler's Guide: Glossary of Terms

cardinal: an official of high rank within the Roman Catholic Church

Cathay: a common term in the Middle Ages for China

Church of the Holy Sepulcher: a church in the city of Jerusalem believed to encompass both the site at which Jesus of Nazareth was crucified and his burial site

delegate: a person authorized to represent the will or the position of another person; in the case of a papal delegate, the will of the pope

Dominican: a member of the Dominican Order, an organization of Catholic preachers founded in 1216 and named for Saint Dominic de Guzman

ducat: a form of currency used in Europe of the Middle Ages

friar: a member of a religious order of men, including the Dominican Order

Genovese: the people of Genoa, a seaport on the northwestern coast of Italy

horde: a group of warriors, often nomadic and traveling by horse

khan: a ruler of the Turkish, Tartar, and Mongol peoples, as well as an emperor of China, during the Middle Ages

khanate: the territory ruled by a khan, or the people within a territory ruled by a khan

Knight Templar: a member of a Christian military order

lama: a spiritual leader, often a Tibetan or Mongol Buddhist monk

Latin: in the Middle Ages, a person native to a territory within the domain of the Roman Catholic Church or a person native to a territory in which the local language derives from the Latin language

Mongol: a group of people native to eastern and central China. In the thirteenth century, the military leader Genghis Khan established a Mongol Empire across central Asia.

Old French: a language predating modern French, which was also used as a common language for elites and merchants in Europe of the Middle Ages

papal: relating to the pope of the Roman Catholic Church

Qara'unas: a Mongol people that settled in the territory later known as Afghanistan

Silk Road: a network of trade routes reaching from China to the Mediterranean Sea

St. John d'Acre: a city in Israel along the coast of the Mediterranean Sea, presently known as Acre. Control over this city was contested throughout the Middle Ages, and it was referred to as St. John d'Acre while under Christian rule.

Tartar: a member of a group of central Asian peoples including both Mongols and Turks

Tartary: a region of Asia and eastern Europe under Tartar control during part of the Middle Ages

Venetian: a person of Venice, a city in northeastern Italy

About the Author

Marco Tabilio was born in 1987 in Riva del Garda, a town in Italy's Trento Province. A cartoonist, an illustrator, and a video artist, Tabilio has been featured in group exhibitions in Bologna, Venice, Hamburg, and Berlin. His work has also been published in a variety of comics magazines. Tabilio is a graduate of the Academy of Fine Arts in Bologna. He lives and works in Hamburg.

Acknowledgments

Thanks to Alice.

Thanks to my parents, Olimpia and Silvano, and my brother, Riccardo.

Thanks to Simone and Daria.

Thanks to all the friends who have supported me at work but also before and after.

Finally, thanks to Marco Polo, Rustichello da Pisa, and to all others.